M000098529

S.K. Grunin is a retired law enforcement officer and a retired college professor. For almost 20 years she taught for the University of Virginia and for a number of other colleges and universities. In addition, Dr. Grunin authored a published text book that was used for her UVA Graduate School courses. Finally, she is a retired Executive, who has also been an Executive Coach, a CEO, a Human Capital Consultant and retired from the Federal Government, where she served in various positions for the Federal Courts, including over 25 plus years spent as a Federal Law Enforcement Officer. Dr. Grunin is a member of the Executive Board of the Gulf Coast Writers Association of SW Florida.

Book 1 of *Little MisFit* is the first in a series of seven books that Dr. Grunin is in the process of writing. Each of these books focus on an important life lesson. In book 2, the Life Lesson is: *"Life Isn't Always Fair"* In addition to writing books, Dr. Grunin is an artist too and she paints oil paintings. Pictures of her paintings and some of her other book titles can be found online.

She and her husband, Howard, have two sons, Jason and Justin. She resides with her husband and their Shiba Inu, Kona, in Naples, Florida.

This book (and other future books in the series) is dedicated to all of us who have at least one time or for one situation in our lives have felt like MisFits. The life lessons are meant to be shared and applied to all of our lives regardless of our age or why we felt like a MisFit; and to help us build confidence, overcome bullying and learn to be successful in how we live our lives.

S.K. Grunin

LIFE LESSONS AND TALES OF LITTLE MISFIT

BOOK 1
LIFE ISN'T ALWAYS WHAT IT SEEMS

AUSTIN MACAULEY PUBLISHERS™

LONDON • CAMBRIDGE • NEW YORK • SHARJAH

A CIP catalogue record for this title is available from the British Library.

ISBN 9781528912280 (Paperback)
ISBN 9781528912297 (Hardback)
ISBN 9781528960076 (ePub e-book)

www.austinmacauley.com

First Published (2020)
Austin Macauley Publishers Ltd
25 Canada Square
Canary Wharf
London
E14 5LQ

To many adults in the world who serve as mentors to help MisFits find their own ways.

Meet Little MisFit
Introduction

Little MisFit often saw herself as someone who didn't quite fit in with most crowds or situations. She didn't find it fun to hang out with the popular kids nor did she find that she could hang out with the nerds or the jocks. Growing up, she was a bright kid, but it took some time for her to find herself and to be sure of who she was. Eventually she knew that she was what adults referred to as a 'Tom Boy'. So let's meet Little MisFit and see what we can learn from her life lessons, tales and how things developed from her point of view and how we all can relate to being a MisFit at times in our own lives. Let's look at what she found as her very first life lesson: *'Life Isn't Always What It Seems'* and see how that might apply to our own lives.

My First Memories

My name is Ivy Sue Klutz. My first memories are of my sister Lynn's five-year-old birthday party – when I was just three and one-half years old. My cousin, Janet, who was about 12 at the time, gathered all of the partygoers in a circle in our living room. I was the youngest one there.

The other guests were my sister's friends from her kindergarten class and some neighbour girls who ranged in age from 5 to 8. After getting our attention, Janet asked if we wanted to play a game. All of the other children began saying, "Oh, yes – yes please."

I just yelled, "Yes." I didn't see any reason to say please since she asked us. Well, unbeknown to me, Janet had told the other party guests that they were not to guess a certain item when the game began. So, as a big truck was backing up into our driveway, Janet asked, "What do you think Lynn is getting for her birthday?"

The kids began guessing, "A doll, a hula hoop, jewellery, a doll house," and on it went.

Well I took one look at the truck and didn't think a truck would be bringing any of those small things so I said, "I know, I know, it's a bike." Well everyone went silent very quickly, and I saw that my cousin was upset and my mom angry as they let me know that I had spoiled my sister's birthday surprise. I could not understand how that was possible since we were asked to guess what Lynn was getting for her birthday, and the truck was right there in front of us in the driveway. Having guessed the right answer, I was expecting a reward and instead my mother yelled me at. As soon as I saw the look on my mother's face, I was able to run and hide while the bike was being rolled off the truck, and everyone else ran outside to see the shiny new bike.

This is my earliest memory; it seemed to me that this, maybe, was why I began to see that things (LIFE) were not always what they seemed. You see, since I was the only one who shouted out that it was a bike, this incident made me feel that I was different from the other kids. As I grew older, I would begin to see that being different was okay, but being different meant that things could also be difficult for me at times. One reason things were difficult was because my parents and teachers always seemed to try to get me to conform. They would say things like, "Why can't you be like your sister or the other kids?"

This was a constant theme in my life – it was even worse when my mother would dress my sister and me in matching outfits – both in pink. I would cry and throw a fit and say how much I hated pink and wanted to wear blue. My mother would say that pink is for girls and blue is for boys. So, I would tell her then to make me a boy. She would just shake her head and say that was not possible. As time went on, I began to see how 'life wasn't always what it seemed'.

Mother also could not understand why I also hated playing house, dress-up and playing with dolls. My sister was always trying to get me to play house or with dolls. She loved dressing up in my mother's fancy clothes. But I refused to play with dolls or dress up unless I could be dad. My mother would just shake her head and say, "Why do you have to be such a Tom Boy?" I wasn't sure what it meant but later I would figure it out.

Well, I couldn't see why I shouldn't be allowed to do the things that I found were fun and, in fact, I soon learned that I liked to do all of the things that boys do. So I was thrilled to learn that I had just gotten a baby brother. He was born right after my sister's fifth birthday. But, at first I was unhappy that I was no longer going to be the baby in the family. I even refused to come to the table and eat dinner with my sister and parents. The only thing that I would do was to sit in my little rocking chair and pout and rock and pout and rock.

Then one day, my mother took us all to visit our family doctor, Dr. Huffton. I didn't like getting shots, but Mother assured me that it was just a checkup visit for my baby brother. Dr. Huffton was a nice older bald man who always gave me a sucker whenever we visited, so knowing that I wasn't getting a shot, I didn't mind going with my mother. My mother told Dr. Huffton that ever since my baby brother was born, I refused to come to the dinner table and eat with the rest of the family. All I would do is sit and pout and rock in my little rocking chair. Dr.

Huffton thought for a minute and then he motioned for me to come over where my baby brother was lying on the table. Next he showed me how my baby brother was different from me and how I was still the baby girl in the family, and he told me that now I would need to be a big sister to my little brother, Tom. After stopping to think for a moment, I thought wow – this is cool as I would take care of and play with my little brother and later, in my mind, I could become a true 'Tom Boy'.

Well, since we had only girls in our neighbourhood and my mother had me promise to play nice and take care of my little brother, my mother now allowed me to help and play with my baby brother. I was elated as I could now play with toys that I thought were much more fun than any that I or my sister had.

So, at Christmas and birthdays, I could hardly wait until my brother opened his presents so we could play with his truck and other toys. My favourite toys were his. Especially his fire truck and the big dump truck that we put rocks and dirt in and play with for hours and hours.

Now, I also hated wearing skirts and dresses. But back when I was in school, I had no choice—we were not allowed to wear pants to school. I was forced to wear skirts and dresses to school and to church. Even in the wintertime when it snowed, we had to wear skirts and dresses with tights underneath. The only day I got a break was on Saturdays when I could wear pants and play ball and run around outside feeling free from those skirts and dresses. I tried to tell my mother that they got in the way of me being able to climb trees and play ball. She would only look at me and say, "That is because girls are NOT supposed to do those kinds of things."

A Surprise Doctor's Visit
at Home

One day my sister came home from school saying that she was sick. She had a lot of spots all over. My mother called Dr. H. and he told her that German measles were going around and that he would come to the house – not to bring my sister to the office.

My brother and I couldn't wait, as we figured this time it would be my sister getting a shot instead of us. It seemed that every time we visited the doctor, we had to get a shot.

So when Dr. H arrived, he took one look at my sister and told my mother to have us come and lay on the couch. We thought that we were going to watch him give my sister a shot. But, boy, were we wrong! Instead, to our surprise, he gave my brother and me a shot and to make matters worse, he didn't even bring any suckers! We always got suckers when we got a shot at the doctor's office. But here we were the healthy ones getting a shot and no sucker. How cruel could he be? Talk about 'life not always being what it seemed'.

I was mad at Dr. H. and I told him so. He said he had to give us a shot to keep us from getting the German measles. I told him that we weren't German – our neighbours were and maybe he was at the wrong house. My mother assured me that he was at the right house and that German was the type of measles that my sister got. I asked if she got them from a German in her class or our German neighbours. The doctor said that anyone could get them or give them – you didn't have to be German – that was just the strain of the disease. I was still mad at our German neighbours (Hyka and Youta) for quite some time, and I told my neighbours just that.

Talk about 'life is not always what it seems'. Let me get this straight, my sister gets sick and my brother and I get shots. My sister, not only did not get a shot, but she got to laugh at us getting the shots. How could this really happen? But it was too weird to make this stuff up.

It was also about this time that the family priest came and blessed our house with holy water. My mother told us that the priest was sprinkling holy water on the floor of each of the rooms. But what my mother did not know was that my brother and I went behind the priest and as soon as he walked into another room, we licked up the holy water.

We thought that the holy water might also make us holy! Boy, would Mother have been mad if she had seen us down on the floor on our hands and knees licking up the holy water. I never even thought that we could end up getting sick from doing such a thing. Now you can begin to see why 'life is not always what it seems' was becoming my theme in life.

Going to School

I couldn't wait to start school. My mother kept telling me, "Just wait enjoy your time at home, as you will be going to school for a long time." Little did I know how right she was, but still, I was bored while my little brother took naps – I didn't have anyone to play with or anything to do. Plus, I just couldn't see the point in taking a nap. Isn't that what sleeping at night was for?

Well, finally the day arrived when I was to go to kindergarten. My mother decided that it would be best if she went with my sister and me and the older neighbour girls who always had walked with my sister to school. It was a large yellow brick building with about a hundred steps leading up to the front door. Also, it was only about eight to ten blocks to the school, but I had only seen it before from our car when we were driving past it.

That morning I didn't even mind putting on a skirt and brushing my hair. I was so excited. The neighbour girls arrived and my mother, with my baby brother in a baby carriage, my sister and I accompanied the girls down the street to the busy street that I had never been allowed to walk across. My mother kept telling me how dangerous this big street was – when we arrived at the corner, I was terrified of the street so I closed my eyes and ran across the street as fast as I could. Apparently, that was the wrong thing to do as cars blew their horns and I could hear my mother screaming. I didn't know what to do so I kept on running. Finally, one of the neighbour girls caught up to me and told me to stop and not to be scared. She explained that there was a crossing guard like a policeman, who stopped the cars so the kids could safely cross the street. Wow – who knew – again, *'Life Isn't Always What It Seems.'*

On my first day of kindergarten, I had to take a nap. Can you believe it – a nap? I had thought that kindergarten was where kids got to play together, read, listen to the teacher read stories and learn stuff. But take a nap – that just seemed wrong as I could do this at home and it was a waste of time, even then I never took a nap at home. What a disappointment this was. I tried to tell my teacher that I didn't even take naps at home and as long as I could remember I didn't take one. She would just point to my towel and tell me to lie down and be quite so the other kids could take a nap. I kept thinking that she thought that she was talking to a dog. Now lie down and be quiet. For me, lying down and being quiet was pure punishment. So, day after day after making sure the teacher was not looking, I would sneak a book off of one of the nearby shelves and look at pictures. Finally, after finding that I did this day after day, as soon as the other kids were settled and resting, the teacher decided to let me go off to another part of the room and look at books.

I found all kinds of cool things in those books and would eventually learn how much fun reading and having books could be. This is an important lesson, but I am getting ahead of my story.

Well, after a few weeks of walking to and from school with my sister and the neighbour girls, one day I came out of school to the place where I was supposed to meet my big sister and her friends to walk home. When I got there, no one was around – not my sister – nor any of the neighbourhood girls, nor any of my sister's friends. I looked around and waited and waited and waited.

After a while, I went back into the school and tried to find my sister's classroom. I wasn't exactly sure where it was as I had never been to it because she always dropped me off in my classroom before going off to hers. But, I did know that first grade classrooms were on the first floor, same as my classroom. But no, no one was there, not even the teacher. When I heard someone coming, I hid behind the big door that led to the outside front steps of the building.

It turned out to be the janitor or the man with the keys as I called him. He was locking all of the doors. I panicked, as I did not want to be locked in the school and have to spend the night here. I didn't think that there was any food anywhere inside and I was getting hungry. So I ran outside to the front steps before he could lock the door and lock me inside the school. I could just picture myself all alone in this big building, and I wanted no part of it.

After waiting a few minutes outside on the front steps, I heard my mother calling me. My mother was in a strange car with my sister. You see, my sister had arrived home with her friends. They had all gone to the candy store after school and had forgotten about me. You couldn't believe how mad I was at my sister for picking candy over waiting for me to walk home with her and her friends. My mother made my sister give me some of the candy that she had gotten when she went to the candy store and forgot to meet me to escort me home. Because of being left at school, the candy didn't make me feel better nor did it taste as good as it usually did. It also made me think again that 'Life Isn't Always What It Seems.'

Well I was glad to finish kindergarten when I learned that first grade was all-day and not just a half-day of school. I also heard from my sister that there wasn't any naptime. Hurrah! Now I could really go to school to have fun, read books and learn.

Moving to the Country

However, on the last day of school as Kindergarten was coming to an end; I was excited to learn that we were moving to the country to live on a farm. I had read a number of books about farm animals and dogs and cats. I just knew that I could be more myself living in the county and that it would be easier to be a 'Tom Boy' living on a farm. It turned out that it was much more fun than I could have imagined.

In the country, I discovered that we still had to wear skirts and dresses to school, but I learned how to not let them get in my way of sword fighting with the boys, climbing trees and having snow ball fights in the snow forts that we built. I also learned that having a sense of humour and making the other kids laugh was seen as being cool. So I decided to try my hand at being a prankster. I thought that this might help me to be more accepted by the other kids.

My first prank involved my name. On the first day of first grade, my teacher asked us to stand up and tell her our first and last names. I decided to use just my initials with my last name. So, when the teacher pointed to me I said, "My name is I.S. Klutz."

The teacher looked at me and said, "I.S. Klutz," and I said, "You too?" Well the other kids all broke out into laughter as they realized that I was saying that the teacher was a klutz. Now that didn't sit too well with this teacher; she was very old and couldn't hear too well, so when she asked what was so funny, I said that I was just repeating my name.

Now this school was almost the opposite of my huge city Kindergarten school, as the country school was a one-room schoolhouse with no one around but the kids in my class and our teacher. I also learned that at recess we got to go outside and play and that the playground was all ours to play on. There were so many things to do and lots of things to climb on – from jungle gyms, slides, merry-go-rounds, swings and lots of trees. Wow! What a cool place to go to school.

Well, I continued to learn that 'Life wasn't always what it seems', as on the first day our teacher told us that we could not climb up the trees. What? They were perfect for climbing, especially the large Oak tree out front. She said that she did not want us falling out of the trees and busting our noggins. We were only allowed to climb up on the playground equipment.

After a few weeks, I decided that God made the trees to be climbed – so up I went. Wow – what a view of the world. Of course, once again, I was different – I was the only one who climbed up into the trees. And, I knew that someone had told the teacher I had done so. This was because after we came inside from the morning recess, my teacher asked me to come up to the front of the class. I thought, *Oh boy this can't be a good thing.* So up to the front of the class I went. The teacher asked me if I had climbed up the big tree. I said, "Who me? Now that is a big tree and I am a small girl so do you really think that I could climb that tree?" You see I didn't want to lie to my teacher. The teacher did think that it was an exceptionally tall tree for someone as small as me to climb and since she didn't see me do it, she said that she'd let it go this time, but next time if I broke the rules, she'd have to send a note home to my mother and father telling them what I had done. A few days later, I decided to get back at the kids who had told on me – I called them 'tattle tale' kids.

As recess started, I jumped up from my desk in the back of the room and ran outside and quickly found the stick that I had hidden just outside the front door of the school. I pushed the stick through the round loop where the lock went when the school was closed.

I then ran around to the windows to watch the kids' faces so I could see how sad and mad they'd be when they discovered that they would not be able to go outside and play for recess. What I didn't realize was that since I hadn't let any other kids outside it would become obvious to the teacher that I was the one who had locked the other kids in the school. It didn't help matters that I was the only one outside standing there in a fit of laughter pointing at the kids through the windows inside.

I hadn't quite thought this prank through. I could see and hear our teacher yelling at me from inside the school to let the kids outside for recess. After taking a few spins on the merry-go- round, I realized it was more fun having the other kids outside and that I should have just played a prank on the tattle-tale kids and not on all of the kids. Well, it was too late for that and I figured that I better let them out before everyone got even madder at me. I walked back up to the front of the school and pulled the stick out of the door and opened the door – almost immediately, out poured the kids from the schoolhouse. I wasn't sure what would happen next so I went and hid outside.

When recess was over, I went back in and sat at my desk as if nothing had happened. Well it wasn't long before the teacher was talking to the class. "Now," she was saying, "who was involved in locking the door so that the other kids could not go out to play at recess?" I knew that she had to know that it was me, but I just sat quietly in my seat. Finally, one of the other kids pointed at me and said that Ivy Sue did it.

The teacher looked at me and said, "Well?"

I said, "Well what?"

She said, "Was it you?"

I said, "Yes."

Okay then, we need to think of a fitting punishment. The kids volunteered all kinds of ideas from me standing on my head to being spanked. Then one suggested that I have to stand in the wastebasket after lunch. I knew what that meant and how the kids would make today's after lunch wastebasket even more special than usual.

So after lunch I had to stand in the wastebasket with all of the kids' lunch leftovers: squashed bananas and peels, apple cores, half-eaten peanut butter and jelly sandwiches, and half-full chocolate milk cartons. This punishment lasted about 15–20 minutes as the teacher said that was the amount of time that I had deprived (whatever that meant) the other kids of recess.

After class, the teacher said that she wanted to see me before I got on the school bus. So I went up to her desk and she handed me a note to give to my mother. Considering what went on that day in school, I decided that the note couldn't have any good news in it so as I got off the school bus, I crumpled the note without anyone seeing me do this and threw it in the ditch and walked home.

Later I was thankful that there were no such things as cell phones as my mother surely would have punished me if I had given her the note from my teacher. I also learned that not all pranks get laughs. 'Life isn't what it always seemed' – so I learned that I had better work on my sense of humour and do fewer pranks. I needed to learn how to tell jokes and if I was to do another prank, it was best not to get caught.

Now, living in the country was not at all like living in the city. For one thing, we only had two other neighbour kids to play with for miles around. Both of these kids were girls; one was older than my sister and the other was in between my sister and me in age. But boy were they both tall, and they never wore shoes except to school, when they had to. They also liked to tell jokes and pull pranks on us. They told us when we first moved into the neighbourhood that they thought that we were Chinese. This is because my mother had taken to calling me Sue since I did not like the name Ivy – who wants to be named after a plant?

Whenever dinner was ready and our mother wanted us three kids to come in from playing outside by the barn, she would yell out the window – "Lynn, Sue, Tom dinner is ready." I thought that it was hilarious that our neighbours thought that but my mother didn't take too kindly to the idea when I told her about this. I never understood why.

To me, the best part of living in the country was getting to play outside in the barn or in the woods. There were so many different kinds of birds and animals and plants to see. It was also at this time that I learned that some of the prettiest insects and plants were poisonous so my life lesson that 'Life isn't always what it seems,' often came in handy when I was out in the woods. Furthermore, I also discovered that there were plants that did not appear to be harmful but after touching nettles and some other three leaf plants and breaking out in hives, I quickly figured out what they looked like and avoided them at all costs.

I also became even more upset by this event when I found out that one of the plants that gave me hives that oozed was called 'Poison Ivy'. You see, my mother had told me that I was named after the plant English Ivy, as I guess we were English.

But it turned out neither was true and when I heard about Poison Ivy, I made all of the kids at school to stop calling me Ivy and told them that they could only call me Sue or by my initials, I.S. At that time, I liked being called Sue after the song, 'A Boy Named Sue'. But there were times that I also liked using my initials so no one could tell I was a girl.

Second Grade

Now my struggles with having to wear pink clothes continued until one day, while I was in second grade and I was painting and I accidently spilled the entire jar of green paint down the front of my sweater and skirt. These were both pink and now they turned a different colour. I was elated – my teacher was not and, in fact, she called my mother to come and pick me up from school. I was not happy as I knew my mother would not be pleased when she saw the green paint all over the front of my pink sweater and the bright pink skirt that she had made me to wear to school. Sure enough, my mother was mad and she told me that she probably couldn't get the green paint out and that I would have to wear the sweater and skirt with the paint stains. I was on top of the world. Imagining I didn't have to wear that plain old pink sweater and skirt, but now I could wear it with the green paint stains! My mother could not understand why this made me excited and so happy.

She would just shake her head and say, "Why can't you be like your sister?" Once again, I thought, *Life Isn't Always What It Seems!*

Also, since there were only girls around for miles and no boys to play with, my mother now was begging to let me play boy games with my brother. In order for my brother to learn to play catch, I explained, begged and pleaded, and finally convinced my mother, with my brother's help, that she also had to get me a baseball glove. She was dead set against it but then she decided that my brother needed a newer glove. Thus, my first glove was my uncle's old glove – he had given it to my brother so I got that one and my brother got a new one.

It mattered not to me, as you see, I thought that having a new glove meant it took time to break it in – my mother thought that she was doing my brother a favour by buying him the new glove. But once again I realized that 'Life is not always as it seems', and that my mother was actually doing me the favour by giving me my uncle's broken-in baseball glove. I learned that it takes a while to break-in a baseball glove, and this one had a superb pocket and was so much fun to use. I loved that glove and used it for many years. I will return to more tales about my baseball glove and me later in Book 2.

Now my brother was a great kid so we hung out a lot together and out in the country; that was an okay thing to do. We made up all kinds of games with our bat and balls – including one of my favourite ball games, 'Innie-Iny-Over'. In this game, you had to throw the rubber ball over the house so the other person, in this case my brother, could catch it and then run around the house to tag me before I could get to the other side of the house. The trick was to try to figure out which way the person who caught the ball was coming. I learned that the best way to do this was to climb a tree and watch my brother run around and around the house. After about four or five times of playing the game this way, he figured out that I was watching him from one of the trees. He was so mad – I almost fell out of the tree laughing so hard the first time that he realized that I had been doing this for quite some time.

We also played tag and made up loads of other games so when my uncle gave us a set of boxing gloves we, or rather I, had the time of my life – that is until my brother got bigger and stronger than me, and I decided that I no longer wanted to box. He was mad as he said that now that he was finally able to beat me at boxing, I quit. I told him that was about right.

The Tom Boy Comes Out in the Second and Third Grades

But, lest I forget, the boxing and play sword fighting with my brother, prepared me for taking on the boys at school –especially the bullies. In second and third grades, I decided that the girls had been bullied enough by two particular boys who would pull their hair, lift up and look under their skirts and grab their hair clips. The teachers would just tell the boys, "Now Jimmy (or Larry) that is no way to treat girls and you shouldn't do those things." Jimmy Miller and Larry Iverson would smile and say, "Yes, Ma'am." And then they would go right on doing these things.

Well I learned that they would only listen to those who were tougher than they were – and remember, 'Life is not always what it seems' – so they did not think that I would be one of those who could make them stop their bullying. One day, Larry crawled under the bus seat, where my sister and I were seated together. He was trying to look up our skirts. I took my sister's metal lunch box and clobbered him in the head. This caused quite a scene with blood going everywhere. Larry needed several stitches and was out of school for several days. But at the scene, with kids screaming, the driver stopped the bus and asked who had hit Larry with their lunch box – my sister had said that she did.

My sister took the blame for my clobbering Larry, but all of the other kids knew and they said nothing. The teacher and bus driver could not believe that it was my sister as she had NEVER done such a thing and was ALWAYS so well behaved. They kept asking her, "Are you sure that you did it and not your sister?"

"Well," Lynn said, "Yes," and she got suspended from school for a week. I kept saying how unfair that was since I was the one who had done it and thought that it should have been me at home, playing outdoors for a whole week while the other kids were in school. Again I remembered that 'life isn't always what it seems'.

After Larry was clobbered, his parents told my parents at a teacher's parent meeting, that he had deserved what happened to him and that Lynn shouldn't have been punished. I couldn't agree more, but that was how it went. I wanted to tell everyone that I did it, but my sister thought that I might get kicked out of school since that was not my first offense nor would it be my last.

Now Jimmy still was the biggest bully on the playground where the second and third graders attended this two-room schoolhouse. At recess, the kids were all scared to go to the part of the playground where Jimmy hung out. One day he was picking on one of the smallest girls in the second grade when I went up to him and clobbered him with a hard right in his left eye. What a shiner that turned into!! All of the other kids on the playground started clapping. Jimmy got up to run inside to tell the teacher when all of the other boys stopped him and said if he told, they would all help me to beat him up. So he ended up saying that he had run into a door and gave himself a black eye.

By third grade, I was the champion ruler sword fighter, having beaten all of the boys more than a few times. In fact, in some cases, several boys decided that they could no longer sword fight with me as their parents were tired of buying them new rulers and they would now have to pay for any new rulers from their own allowances. Now these were not your typical plastic rulers, no, they were the solid wooden ones with the metal side. I learned a form of Judo from watching TV that showed me how to quickly demolish the enemy's sword (wooden ruler) and usually I was able to do it before we got into a real sword fight battle.

Well, one day David Irvine got the jump on me in the back of the classroom as I was getting ready to take my seat after recess and was putting my ruler in my desk. I grabbed my ruler but it was too late. David was fighting away, and I was having difficulty keeping him at bay. Finally, I stood on one of the desks and was able to get the upper hand, so to speak. I splintered David's ruler all across the back of the classroom just as our third grade teacher was returning from the bathroom. She was so mad; she was fuming. She said David and I would have to be punished for our behaviour. We just laughed and went back to our seats.

The next week was report card day. This is when your teacher gave you a yellow card to take home with letters for grades. Now all of my grades had been A's and O's, except for a few B's and/or S's in Citizenship but not this time. I stared down at my report card and saw a big 'D' in the line that said Citizenship and then in the notes section, I saw a word that I did not know its meaning. The note read: *Sue is defiant. Please come and see me during teacher-parent meeting.*

I knew that this could not be good news. So at the bus transfer point, where I had to wait about 20 minutes for the bus that would take me home, I went around back of the transfer school and took an ink eraser to the D in the Citizenship grade. Then I got an idea to turn it into a B. But it was too late as the ink eraser had put a hole in the spot where the Citizenship grade was. It also made the card look lighter in colour so I realized that I'd just have to tell my mother that my teacher had made a mistake and changed her mind as to my grade in Citizenship.

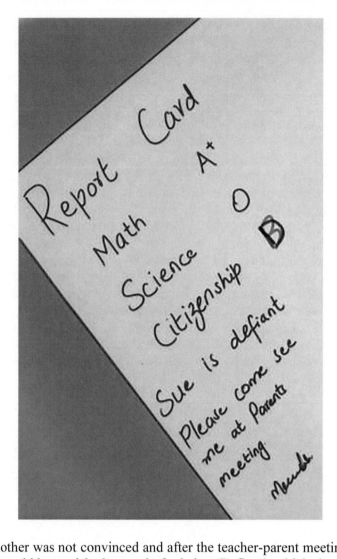

My mother was not convinced and after the teacher-parent meeting she told me that I would be punished not only for being 'Defiant', which she said meant not doing what the teacher said to do, but also for lying to her about the Citizenship grade and for changing the grade on my report card. You can't blame me for trying – I didn't have time to erase the word defiant but since I didn't know what it meant, I thought that I could bluff my way through that one with my mother. But boy was I wrong – my mother knew the meaning of the word, and I had to give up two weeks' allowance and do all of my brother and sister's chores during this time as my punishment for this behaviour.

As the end of third grade was approaching, our class was exceptionally rowdy. Our teacher had given us our assignment and went in back to use the restroom. When she returned, the classroom was in utter chaos with paper airplanes sailing everywhere across the room; some girls playing hop scotch in the cloak room; some boys wrestling, and David and I and a few others having a big sword fight battle with our rulers. Our teacher just threw up her arms, got her purse and put her coat on, and walked out to her car. She got in and by then we were all at the window watching her drive away.

Our third grade class was part of a two-classroom schoolhouse. Hearing the noise in our classroom, the second grade teacher opened the door between the two classrooms and stuck her head in. At this point the chaos had resumed and upon seeing the class in disarray, Mrs. Willett, the second grade teacher, clapped her hands and asked for order. She said that we should all be ashamed of ourselves for driving our teacher away as she too had seen Ms. Seyfridge, our teacher, get in her car and drive away. We told her that we were just having some fun – that went over like a lead balloon.

As it turned out, at the end of that school year, I had not missed one day of school and our third-grade teacher stated that fact helped her to decide to retire from teaching. Who can blame her? We had a glorious year, and I was the sword fighting champion of third grade. Well, we knew that Ms. S was serious about retiring when on the last day of school, she held a raffle and raffled off all of her books and teaching materials to us. We all felt a little embarrassed by this but it was too late to undo the things that we did in her classroom. I won her 'Time for Poetry' book and Ms. S said that she hoped that I would use it to teach and that I would have a class of students similar to the one I was in. I don't think that she meant it as a compliment but rather that I should get payback for how I behaved and have students who were disruptive and unruly as our class had been. I told her that we deserved what she was saying and thanked her for the poetry book and that I would figure out how to use it in my life. I looked through it and didn't find any jokes or any sayings that I thought would be helpful to me in the near future – so onward and upward I went as we broke for summer recess.

Using My Brother as a Guinea Pig to Tell Jokes

I figured that I needed to work on my sense of humour as I thought that would help me with the other kids. Now, my little brother was three grades behind me in school as he was born in January and had to start school later than me, who was born in August. I didn't see how that was fair but then 'life isn't always what it seems'. But since, my brother was small for his age he really didn't mind starting school a little later in life. As I finished third grade, he was finishing Kindergarten half-day school.

Thus, he was always waiting for me at the front door when I came home from school. He could not wait for me to tell him what I did in school – but I decided that I could not tell him all of my adventures, as he had a habit of spilling the beans at dinner time when my parents would ask: "Ivy Sue, what did you do or learn in school today." Can you imagine what my parents would have said if I had said well, today we were so disruptive that our teacher got in her car and left for the rest of the day? The second grade teacher told us that we should be ashamed of ourselves for our behaviour. I was sword fighting with my ruler with two other boys – otherwise, not much happened.

So, I thought that instead of telling him about school, it would be a good idea to tell him jokes that I had heard and let him tell them to see how my parents would react to the jokes, before I tried them out on others. My brother, Tom, really liked telling the jokes as most times my mother and father and sister would laugh. But, on occasion, my mother and father would glare at me and say, "Now, Ivy Sue, wherever did you learn that joke?"

I would just shrug and say, "From school."

"Well, who are you hanging out with? Sounds like they are not a good influence on you."

From that I learned which boys' jokes not to tell my little brother.

I also got my brother to learn several jokes and to practice telling them. Then when all of my aunts and uncles and cousins would come over, my brother would stand up and tell the jokes that I had taught him. He enjoyed the attention, even though he didn't know what half of the jokes that he told meant. At the end of his joke time, my Aunt Jenny would ask him if he wanted to be a comedian when he grows up and that's when I whispered to him to say, "No, I want to be a Mexican." That probably got the most laughs even though my brother didn't even know what a Mexican was.

Going to the Big School–Fourth Grade and Getting Put in Charge of My Class

I found myself in a very different place when it came time to go to fourth grade. You see, unlike first, second, third, fifth and sixth grades, fourth graders had to attend the big school. I also discovered that there weren't any one-room schoolhouses for fourth graders. I am not certain why this was the case, but it was also challenging to learn that our fourth grade teacher, Mrs. Lynch, was also the principal of the school. We learned what that meant was that she was in charge of the whole school. Most of us had not attended a school with a principal before – I am certain that my Kindergarten school in the city had a principal but I was too young to have met her or him.

I also learned that Mrs. Lynch took no prisoners. She was tough like her namesake. I liked that. Also, she had heard of our third grade class' reputation for being disruptive and had spoken with our teacher who had indeed retired from teaching. So I was surprised when the first time that she had to leave the classroom, she told our class that Ivy Sue would be in charge and that all of the other students had to listen to me and do what I asked them to do. She told me what the lesson was, handed me the wooden pointer and walked out of the room. Hot dog – what a situation to be put in.

Now, as soon as the door was shut, I knew that the kids would test me. First, David jumped up from his seat with his ruler and tried to sword fight with another boy. I put an end to this quickly as I took the ruler from him. You see, once he saw me holding the wooden pointer over his head, he didn't dare challenge me to see if I would have used it on his head. He didn't want to chance it, as he knew that I didn't take any gruff from the other kids – including the bullies. So the other students decided it was best to go ahead with the geography lesson that the teacher had told me to lead.

As I went home that night, I again realized that I was different but this time it felt okay to be different, and that I didn't mind being the teacher's pet as long as I was respected by both the teacher/principal and the other students. This was a new experience for me. Again, 'life isn't always what it seemed', was what I was learning.

As time went by, I was always Mrs. Lynch's choice to be the one that she put in charge of the class whenever she was called out to handle a situation, which turned out to be several times a day. I figured that Mrs. Lynch must have decided that by putting me in charge, she took care of the most disruptive student and that I had the respect and capability to run the classroom better than any other student. After all, I knew who the problems were and how to handle them.

Things went smoothly after that, but I found out that I was again different when it came to our music classes and music teacher. First, he asked us to skip. I had no clue what he meant by skipping, and worse yet, I could not figure out how to put my feet together to skip. You see, I had never skipped before. I just couldn't make it happen. I was sooo frustrated!

This is also when I realized that my namesake – Klutz – was coming home to haunt me. To make matters worse, I not only could not skip, but I also had difficulty trying to hold any rhythm or a tune. The music teacher had us sing a song – Little Bird in the Kapok Tree – no one would try to sing the tune, as we had never had music before in school. I stepped up and sung the tune. I am certain that I missed most, if not all of the notes. But, the music teacher awarded me first chair because no one else had attempted to do it. Well, it wasn't long until I was close to being last chair in the class as the other kids began to use their vocal cords and demonstrate that they could carry a tune. Having seen me attempt the tune, they all came forward and were far superior to me in singing the song. But, I also saw how being the first one to try something was not a bad thing.

Being Called 'Clumsy'

Well, my namesake seemed to keep making things even worse for me as the day arrived that my mother referred to me as clumsy. You see, I had just carried the laundry basket outside and I dropped it. The laundry basket was full to the top with the clean wash and it spilled out all over the grass in the backyard. Hanging up the laundry was my chore; I never figured out why my sister never had to help with hanging up the laundry; it had something to do with ruining her nails as I remember.

Now, I had not heard the word, 'clumsy' before then. At school, later that week, I looked up the word 'clumsy' and saw the word, 'klutz' and then found the definition to be, 'a clumsy, awkward person'. Wow – here my namesake was coming true to life. I had no idea that Klutz had that bad of a definition. I just knew that the kids had thought it was funny when I used my initials with my last name, 'I.S. Klutz'.

I went home that day from school and asked my mother how we got the name Klutz. She said it was our father's last name and that he had grown up with it. I asked her if he had the same problems that I was having with it and she said no. WOW. What to do? My mother suggested that I take dancing lessons to give me more balance and poise – whatever that was.

I hated the idea of taking dancing lessons – especially ballet. Really? Me in a tutu with ballerina slippers – what a joke! Well my sister loved the idea and my mother was convinced that this would help me feel less clumsy and less different than the other kids – especially the girls. Also, my mother was concerned that all of my best friends were boys and that taking dancing lessons might help me make more friends who were girls.

Well that didn't happen. First, I made friends with Jeff Underhill, who was great at dancing and he showed me several dance steps, which I had extreme difficulty with.

But I told my mother that I would take dancing lessons, if I wouldn't have to wear a tutu, especially a pink one. Well that lasted about a week or so. You see, initially my mother had kept her word and had bought me a blue outfit and my sister a pink one. But one day during our lessons my sister had an accident and peed in her outfit in our dance class.

I was so embarrassed, but to make matters worse, from that day on, my sister got to wear my blue dance outfit while I had to wear the pink one that she peed in. Can you believe this? Talk about 'Life Isn't Always What It Seems'.

Well, after a while, I convinced my mother, with the dancing teacher's help, that I should drop ballet lessons and just continue with the tap-dancing lessons. I liked the noises that the tap shoes made when I walked down the hall with them. I also felt that I could survive the tap lessons and I wouldn't have to wear the pink 'froufrou' outfit again.

The most fun part of the tap lessons was that our group was going to do a dance recital called 'The Horse with the Lavender Eyes'. I was excited as I was given the part of being the back end of the horse. My teacher said that she thought that I couldn't mess that part up. I thought that this was a compliment and was excited to get to dress up as the back part of the horse. So after a number of weeks of practice, recital day arrived. My parents and all of these people showed up and were in the audience of the auditorium where we had practiced on the stage for the past few months.

After getting into our costumes, I was led out behind another girl who played the front part of the horse, and I was told just to follow her lead. Well, I don't know how one is supposed to do that when you're the behind in the horse costume and can't see the feet of the front of the horse. So as the music got going, I decided to give it my all and began dancing up a storm as the back of the horse.

I couldn't see anything but I did hear a lot of laughter and clapping so I guessed that things were going smoothly and decided to take a little license and take the lead and dance around the front of the horse. I understand that the audience found it hilarious but not so my dancing teacher, nor some of the parents of some of the other girls. 'Life isn't always what it seems'.

Later, I was to learn that 'The Horse with the Lavender Eyes' was supposed to be a horse for a Merry-go-round and that I was just supposed to stand still while the girl in the front went up and down and danced some steps. Obviously that was not how I saw things from my position. Yep, you guessed it, that was my one and only dance recital!

Clay-Its – Trying to Use Creativity in Another Endeavor (and Make Some Money)

Well, I had to find something else to occupy my time. Sometimes being out in the country you had to make up your own entertainment and fun. We didn't have a lot of games and there were no such things as computers and iPads back then. So, we looked around and saw that the one thing we had a lot of was mud. Now, this mud was a form of clay and we discovered that we could actually make things out of it.

I got the idea for us to make paperweights and then make a sign, and take them to the busy road about a mile away and sell them. So after we made a half dozen or so of 'Mallard Ducks' that we painted green with some poster paint that I found in the basement from another school craft project, we were ready to sell our creations. I made a sign that said, *Clay-Its 4 Sale.*

My sister put the 'clay-its' in the basket on the front of her bike. My brother brought some change, in case people needed change from dollar bills as we were going to charge 50 cents per 'clay-it', and I carried the sign on my bike as we got ready for our big moment.

As the three of us kids were preparing to ride our bikes down the road to the paved highway, my mother happened to look out the window. She was aghast and could not believe her eyes. She ran outside saying, "What are you kids doing?" We explained that we were trying to make some money selling paperweights.

She said that she would buy them all from us. Later we found out that she was so embarrassed by our efforts. Furthermore, she did not want any of our neighbours seeing what were we're up to, and that is why she bought them all. What a bummer!

After this she made us promise not to make any more and she said that if we wanted to earn some money, she would pay us for picking up pieces of glass and nails from our driveway. Apparently, the old farmhouse that had been on this site had burned to the ground and it had left a lot of nails and glass around the area where our driveway was located. This often resulted in our car getting a flat tire that my dad would have to fix.

While I was picking up the pieces of glass, I got the bright idea to break some of the bigger pieces of glass into smaller pieces in order to make more money. That is, I did this until my mother caught us and then she said she'd only pay us for the glass if it weren't broken into smaller pieces. 'Life isn't always what it seems.'

Mrs. Martin – Our 90-Year-Old Neighbour

I think that I forgot to mention that the farm that we now lived on was one of the farms that my father grew up on.

This is important because my 90-year-old neighbour, Mrs. Martin, remembered my father when he was a little boy. She would tell me stories about him walking the horses pulling the ploughs in the field. She said that my dad was a real 'stinker', and he used to play tricks on everyone. Maybe this is where I got my personality.

I loved listening to her stories every time I would stop by to visit her. She had lived on her farm all of her life. She was of American Indian heritage and she explained how her father 'homesteaded' their farm when he was young. Her farmland was given to her father and his family as a way to end the fights between the Chippewa Indians and the American federal government. She said that she was a little girl when her father built their farmhouse.

Their house was very small with only three rooms; a bedroom, a living room and a kitchen that had been added on later after the house was first built. Also, it had no indoor plumbing and the cooking stove was a fire pit over a fireplace, which also served as the only source of heat for the house.

I became very fond of Mrs. Martin, and when I learned that she lived alone and seldom did her children or grandchildren visit, I made it a point to visit her each week. I also would take her 'SS' check down to the corner store and get it cashed for her (where she had an account and they knew her) and I would get her groceries and also carry in water from the back well. Her water was gotten through a pump and she also had an outdoor outhouse.

One day, I rode my bike down to Mrs. M's farmhouse and saw her outside in her rocking chair, sitting on her front porch. I rode up to the porch and called out to her, "Hello Mrs. Martin, can I do anything for you today?" She motioned for me to come into the house with her. I got off my bike and went inside. I waited by her front door and a few minutes later, she came over to where I was standing and brought over a box. Her eyesight wasn't very good. She asked me what it was, and she said that it tasted soapy.

I looked at the box and said that it was laundry soap. In big letters, the word, PUNCH was found on the front of the box.

She looked at me in surprise and said, "Funny name for laundry soap!" I could see her point and again I thought, *Life Isn't Always What It Seems.* I agreed with her and told her not to drink anymore. She laughed and said that she would not as it tasted terrible. I just laughed, but I thought, *Gee, I wonder if companies even give any thought to naming products things that have a double meaning and how this impacts people who don't have great eyesight like Mrs. Martin.* (After this event, I would visit Mrs. Martin almost every week that I was at home until I went away to college).

One thing that I thought that I might be able to do for her was to paint her porch and the front of her house. So one day I surprised her and brought over a 5 gallon bucket of white paint. I asked her if it'd be okay if I painted her porch and the front of her house for her.

She broke out into tears and said not even her son had offered to do that for her. It took my sister and me several weeks to paint the porch and the front of her house, but we did it and boy was Mrs. Martin thankful. She even gave me an old rhinestone brooch. Not that I ever wore it but I kept it for sentimental reasons.

End of Fourth Grade

As I finished fourth grade, I had learned a lot about how 'Life Isn't Always What It Seemed'. For starters, I had learned that one had to look behind what one saw to understand what was really happening. The saying, 'You can't judge a book by its cover,' really fit this life lesson.

I also had discovered how much I enjoyed reading books and finding how much they could take one into another world. I saw books as a lifeline for those of us who couldn't travel or have money to try new experiences. They helped us to learn about nature, other countries and cultures, about philosophy and about adventures and life lessons themselves. They brought joy, sorrow and excitement into my life.

By this point in time, I had also read every Nancy Drew book that I could get my hands on. I saw myself as Nancy Drew trying to solve the mysteries and crimes that she was trying to solve. She was quite a sleuth. I also thought how fun it would be to be a sleuth in real life and wondered what kind of career path that I might want to follow.

As I had discovered back in the second grade, the bookmobile still provided a great source for us country kids to be able to access books. I was concerned about not being able to have the bookmobile during the upcoming summer. I discussed this with the woman who ran the bookmobile. She told me that during the summer, my mother could bring me to the town library where she would make sure that I could check out books to read and have them over the entire summer. I was thrilled.

I had my mother take me once a week, where I proceeded to check out as many books that I could at one time.

I was allowed to check out four books each visit to the library. I even got my very own library card.

I found that the books took me on trips and adventures that I never even dreamed existed. I also discovered, through reading dozens of books, that not judging a book by its cover was exactly like 'Life Isn't What It Always Seems'. In fact some of the most exciting books often did not have pictures on their covers – only words.

Through books, I learned that travel and nature books provided me with new knowledge and an excitement about life that I did not know was there. Through my summer of fourth grade, I visited many countries and found how people lived so very differently from me and how they spoke different languages and dressed differently. This also helped me to realize that it was okay to be different from others.

I found that nature books gave me insight into how magnificent nature was. I learned how lightning bugs really worked and how bees made honey. I learned the difference between beetles and bugs and this got me interested in starting an insect collection. I would spend hours collecting, mounting and studying these various insects. At one point, I had over 175 different insects in my collection.

I also learned how Science was there to help us appreciate the world around us and how God helped us to be thankful for what we had and that it was important to take care of our earth, our home. In other words, as a farmer would say, I learned how important it is to look under the hood of a car and see what is there and not just look at the shiny chrome of the car's exterior.

It was at this time that I began to realize that school was more than just play; it was also a place to learn about our world. This got me really excited about heading to fifth grade. This was also the year of going back to a one-room schoolhouse, the one closest to my farmhouse. It was also to be a school year that I would remember for the rest of my life.

Book 2 is where you will find more tales of me in fifth grade, where I learned my next life lesson: 'Life Isn't Always Fair.' This life lesson taught me how to deal with life when it is not fair and how to make the best of bad situations when they occur. I think that it was one of the best life lessons that I have ever learned and I still use it to this day!